To my #Tribe, and to all the tribes who, between tribes and tribes, knock down walls, design bridges, and erase borders.

—S. I. G.

To my wife and our children, my refuge

—S. N.

Text by Sandra le Guen
Illustrations by Stéphane Nicolet

Previously published as *Refuge* by Éditions les P'tits Bérets in France in 2019. Translated from French by Daniel Hahn.
First published in English by Amazon Crossing Kids in collaboration with Amazon Crossing in 2020.

Published by Amazon Crossing Kids, New York, in collaboration with Amazon Crossing
www.apub.com

ISBN-13: 9781542020503 (hardcover)
ISBN-10: 1542020506 (hardcover)

The illustrations were rendered digitally.

Book design by Tanya Ross-Hughes
Printed in China

First Edition

10 9 8 7 6 5 4 3 2 1

The Refuge

by Sandra le Guen

illustrated by Stéphane Nicolet

translated by Daniel Hahn

When Jeannette got home from school that day, she dropped her bag on the floor. She didn't bother to take off her shoes, and she didn't bother to have her afternoon snack.

When Jeannette got home from school that day, she hurried into her mom's office. She opened the window wide. She pointed the telescope toward the sky and brought her eye up close.

"What are you looking at, Jeannette?"
her mom asked.

"I'm trying to see where the stars go in the daytime to hide."

"The daylight makes them invisible to the naked eye—that's true,"
said her mom. "But they are always there."

"There's a new girl at school. She never stops looking up at the sky!
She likes the stars and comets.
She draws meteors and planets."

"She has big green eyes.
They get a bit wet sometimes.
Her mouth doesn't smile much—"

"It's not always easy changing schools," Jeannette's mom interrupted her.
"Why don't you find out if she'd like to play with you?"

The next day at recess, Jeannette and the new girl looked up at the sky together.
The new girl didn't know the language very well.
She pointed with a finger.
She used her hands to explain.

The teacher had given her some chalk and
a board, some felt-tip pens, and pictures.
The new girl told Jeannette stories—using gestures,
and funny faces, and drawing on the ground.
Jeannette asked questions—using words,
and gestures, and drawing on the ground.

They chattered away for the whole recess.
It was all over too fast!

Then they said—see you tomorrow for more,
and the day after tomorrow, too.

Now in class they exchanged smiles and
a little wave from time to time.

Jeannette, in turn,
explained to her parents.

The new girl changed her country. She changed her life. She traveled across the sea with her dad, her mom, and her little sister. There were so many of them on such a small boat.

"In their country there's a war," Jeannette said. "Her family had no choice. Did you know her dad was a doctor?"

"No, we didn't know. You haven't told us her name, either."

"It's Iliana. To us this sounds like a nice easy journey. Not to her. She told me."

It took her parents a while to decide to leave it all behind. They needed a lot of money, too. Money to pay the smugglers who brought them, money to pay for the crossing, money to pay for the life vests.

On the boat, Iliana was so, so scared. She held her mom's hand tight, never letting go. Her little sister was in their dad's arms. Iliana's mom told her to look up at the sky she loved so much. The changing moon, the twinkling stars, the clouds you can see in the daytime and just barely make out in the night.

It was very tough.
Waves crashed onto the boat.
The sun crashed onto her head.

She said she was very cold anyway.
And hungry.
And thirsty.
To help her try to forget, she had her mom's arms around her and the sky to look at.

With the North Star as her compass, she traced the path of that long and dangerous journey.

"Her mom told her that the sky belonged to everybody,"
Jeannette said, "and that there were no borders.
And that when she arrived here, she'd be able to keep studying
just like she had back there. Did I tell you her grandpa was
a doctor, too? That's why he stayed in their country.
To help the wounded, and to look after—"

"No, you didn't tell us. . . .
Do you want to invite Iliana to come over?"

Iliana accepted the invitation.

It was an emotional meeting for the two families.
Iliana's parents brought some very sweet homemade
pastries for everyone to have with their tea.

Now it was their turn to talk. They spoke English very well
and a few words of French. They talked about arriving on this side of the sea,
the barbed wire, the policemen. The long hours of walking. The hunger,
the cold, the tiredness, the fears, the tears they couldn't help from falling,
the great crossing, the shouting, the wounds on their feet . . .

And then, the meetings with the people from the organizations, the smiles,
the warmth, the care. The words *asylum*, *reception*, *welcome* being spoken at last.
Such a long time coming.

Jeannette showed Iliana the telescope. The two children gazed up at the sky.
The movement of the clouds, their shapes changing as they traveled.
Iliana said their names in her language.

Then they went all the way down to the end of the garden,
to the tree house perched in the great oak.

"Iliana loved it. She said it was such a cool refuge.
And she really wants to go up there one night to look at the stars!
Could we have that adventure sometime, Mom, could we?"

And so it was that one night, the two children gazed up at the twinkling stars and the full moon. They stared at the craters. They looked for the constellations beginning with the North Star. They saw meteors, too, and their bursts of light!

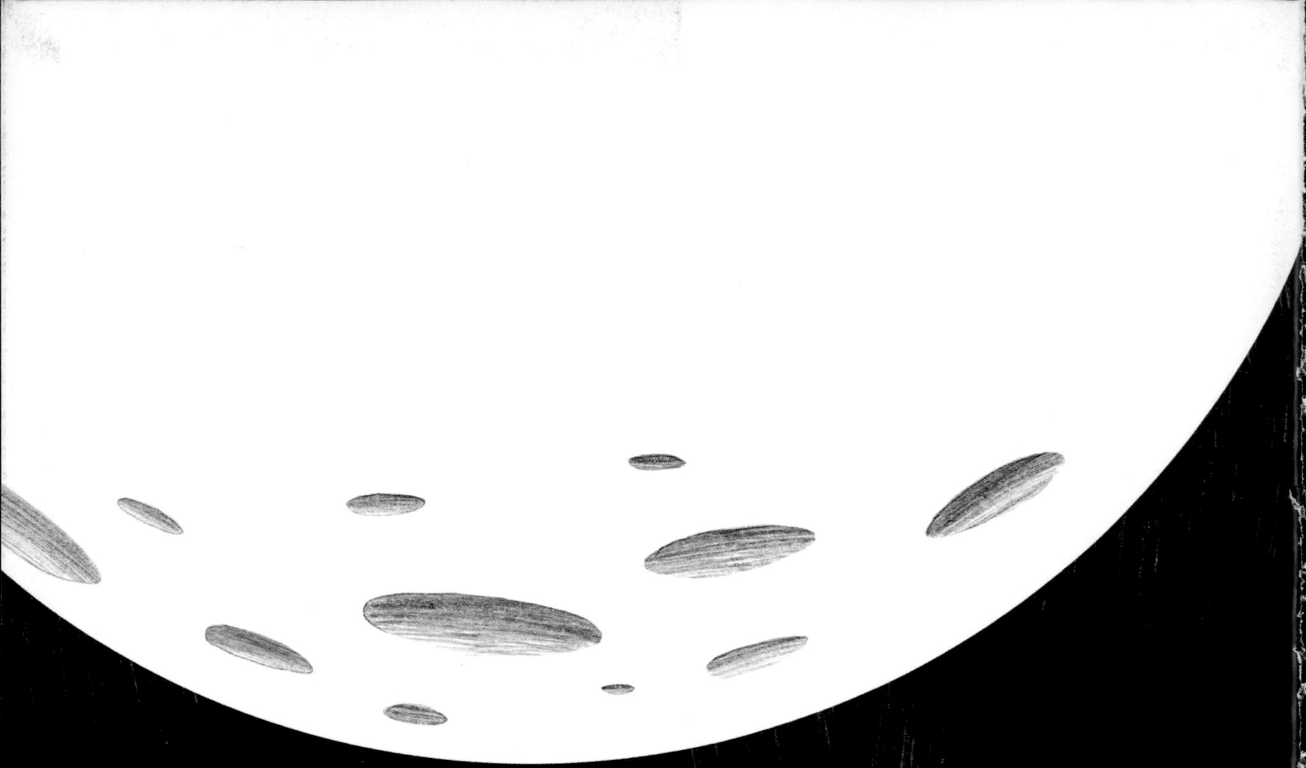

Jeannette told her parents: “Iliana says the sky is a refuge for everybody. No barriers, no borders. She’s taught me some songs from her country. She told me when she grows up she’s going to be an astronaut, to get as close to the stars as she can. She’s going to study physics, chemistry, and math.

“And I told her I will, too.”

Jeannette and Iliana used their fingers to draw a hopscotch pattern in the night. And then they tossed tiny pebbles—1, 2, 3—up into the sky!

They pretended to catch the stars in a butterfly net, and they gave them names. They laughed, they smiled, and then they fell asleep, sheltered and safe.

ciel
7
8
6
4
5
3
2
1

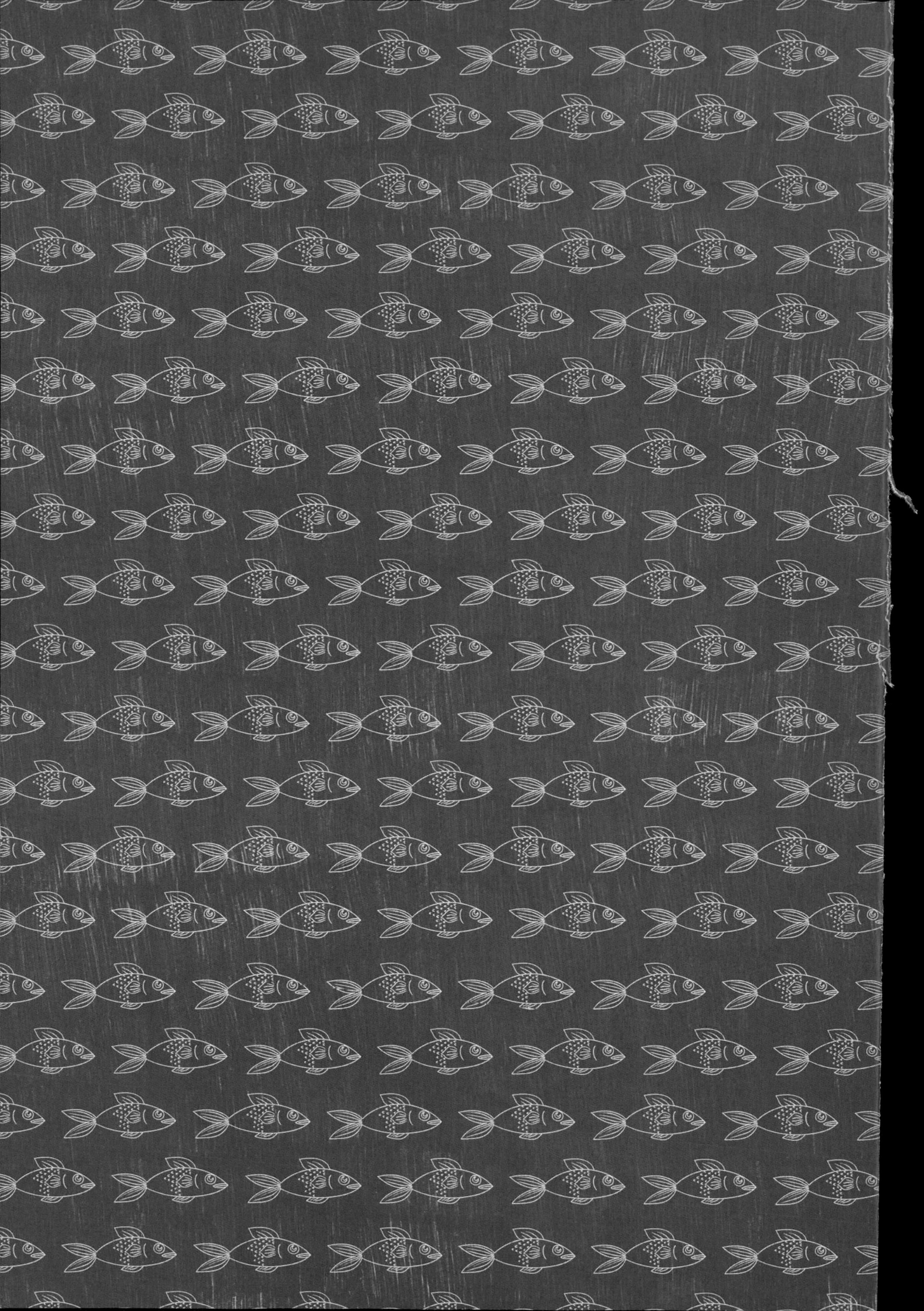